DATE DUE 4/18

PRINTED IN U.S.A.

SURVIVOR DIARIES

OVERBOARD!

SURVIVOR DIARIES

OVERBOARD!

BY TERRY LYNN JOHNSON

HOUGHTON MIFFLIN HARCOURT
Boston   New York

www.hmhco.com

The text was set in Adobe Caslon Pro.
Illustrations by Jani Orban

Library of Congress Cataloging-in-Publication Data
Names: Johnson, Terry Lynn, author.
Title: Overboard / by Terry Lynn Johnson ; with illustrations by Jovan Ukropina.
Description: Boston ; New York : Houghton Mifflin Harcourt, [2017]. | Series: Survivor diaries ; [book 1] | Summary: Eleven-year-old Travis and twelve-year-old Marina, separated from their families after being thrown into the Atlantic off the coast of Washington, battle hypothermia as they struggle to survive. Includes Coast Guard-approved cold-water survival tips.
Identifiers: LCCN 2016028377 | ISBN 9780544970106 (hardback)
Subjects: | CYAC: Survival—Fiction. | Lost children—Fiction. | Atlantic Ocean—Fiction. | BISAC: JUVENILE FICTION / Action & Adventure / Survival Stories. | JUVENILE FICTION / Nature & the Natural World / Environment. | JUVENILE FICTION / People & Places / United States / General. | JUVENILE FICTION / Animals / Marine Life.
Classification: LCC PZ7.J63835 Ove 2017 | DDC [Fic]—dc23
LC record available at https://lccn.loc.gov/2016028377

Manufactured in the United States of America
DOC 10 9 8 7 6 5 4 3 2
4500671567

For my fellow officers in the marine unit, past and present. I've learned so much from all of you.

CHAPTER ONE

"Tell me how you survived the whale attack," the reporter said.

Not this again. I sank back into the couch cushions and rubbed my face.

"That's not the real story," I told him. I could hardly believe what had actually happened.

He leaned in. "Then tell me the real story. That's why I'm here. As I explained, I'm writing a series about survivors—kids like you—who made it home alive after a life-threatening experience. I want to hear about that afternoon while you were on vacation. You and Marina were the only ones who didn't make it to the life rafts."

He glanced over his shoulder toward the kitchen. The smell of peanut butter cookies drifted toward us.

"I want to hear the truth so young people who read these survivor diaries can learn from you. There aren't many eleven-year-olds who've had an experience like yours."

He placed his phone on the coffee table between us and pressed Record. "So, Travis, how did you survive?"

I stared at the bald man sitting in my living room. He was asking me to talk about the worst moments of my life.

I blew out a breath. "I didn't even know what was going on at first. Marina just yelled the warning and then the next thing you know I'm in the water. Everything was crazy loud. You know that bubbly kind of sound you hear underwater? Except not the peaceful kind like when you're swimming. It was even worse on the surface with the waves smacking me in the face and the wind howling and people screaming and . . ."

"No, no." He scratched at his tiny beard on his chin. "I want you to start at the beginning. The whole story. Take your time."

I took a sip from my lemonade. "It all started with the whales."

CHAPTER TWO

Four months earlier

The boat swayed beneath me. I spread my feet apart to balance and lifted my face into the wind. It smelled like seaweed and salt and some kind of animal poop and it was awesome.

"Put this on, Trav." Mom ambushed me with a red and black suit. She held it open for me to step into like I was five, and stuffed my arm into a sleeve.

"What? No, what is that?"

"An immersion suit. It's rough today, and it's going to be chilly on the water."

"Stacey's not wearing one," I said.

"Older. And wiser." My sister didn't look up from texting, but she smirked for my benefit.

I let Mom do up the zipper—no point in arguing. Ever since my gym accident, Mom had been hovering. It was my life.

"And I hid some animal crackers in the pocket in case you want a snack."

"Mom," Stacey said. "I think the last thing Chunky Monkey needs is a snack."

"Welcome aboard the *Selkie Two*," a man said through the speakers attached to the outside of the cabin.

The *wheelhouse* is what Dad had called it. I could see inside through the big windows to where people were sitting on benches.

"I'm your captain, Alfonso Hernandez. My daughter Marina and I are happy you've chosen to come with us this afternoon. July is a great time for whale watching in the Strait of Juan de Fuca."

The captain was talking into a microphone while steering the boat from the front of the cabin. A dark-haired girl next to him waved.

"For the next three hours, we hope to find you some harbor seals and sea lions. If we're lucky we'll see orcas, and maybe humpbacks. There's a ten-knot northwest wind, we'll have a bit of chop, but nothing our fine vessel can't handle. Let's hope the wildlife cooperates. We do guarantee jellyfish sightings."

Someone standing next to me at the railing chuckled.

"So let's get to the introduction, and then we'll be all set. We've got twenty-three on board today, including crew. This is a fifty-foot vessel equipped with all the latest safety features."

I watched the girl, Marina, through the giant windows. She walked through the cabin pointing at things as her dad talked about where everything was.

My focus drifted back to the water. White lines raced across the surface. Rolling waves curled at their tops. The waves slapped against the boat as we headed out, directly toward the mountains in the background. I couldn't believe we were finally here.

"Think we'll see a whale?" I asked Dad.

Out of everything we had planned on our vacation to Washington State, this was what I'd been looking forward to the most. I'd never seen a whale.

Dad's knuckles whitened as he gripped the rail. "Uh . . . er . . . maybe. I think I should go sit for a bit. You keep watch." He was pale already and we'd just started.

"Aren't those magic bands working?" I asked, pointing to what he wore on his wrists to stop seasickness.

"Come on, Travis," Mom said. "We'll all go inside."

"But I want to see the whales," I said. "Look, I've got my suit on."

"Leave him be, Mandy," said Dad, as he lurched toward the cabin.

"I'm going up," Stacey said, and she headed for the stairs to the platform on top of the cabin. "Better cell reception."

I started to follow but Mom pulled me back. "No, I don't want you to slip."

Once I got closer to the stairs, I could see Mom was right. They were steep, and that platform looked high. I was glad she'd said no, but I pretended to be disappointed.

Mom glanced back at me with worried eyes before she helped Dad into the cabin. I walked to the other side of the boat.

Freedom! The wind blew through my hair. With the suit on, I wasn't cold at all.

"Harbor porpoises!" a voice said beside me.

I turned and saw Marina pointing out into the water. Her wide-brimmed hat was attached with a chin strap. A blue-checkered bandanna flapped around her neck, making her look like an adventurer from a magazine.

"There's a pod of them following the current line! Do you see?"

I searched the water and saw nothing but waves.

"You can tell they're harbor porpoises because their dorsal fins are shaped like chocolate chips."

A small black fin popped out of the water and dipped back in again.

"There! I saw it," I said. "They swim so fast." I looked at her and grinned.

She wore a short red life jacket over her Windbreaker. The life jacket had things attached to it, including a small knife sheath.

"That's cool," I said, pointing to the knife.

"It's my marine knife. I always keep it on my guide vest. All mariners wear them in case we have to cut a line real quick."

"You're a guide? How old are you?"

"Twelve. But you don't have to be old to know stuff. I've been doing this my whole life."

I tried to think of a way to change the subject because I didn't want her to ask how old *I* was next and find out that I was younger than her. But she wasn't looking at me; she was gazing across the waves.

I followed her gaze and saw what she was looking at. More fins sticking out of the water, but these were long. Some of them looked as tall as Mom.

Marina waved to her dad through the window and pointed.

"J-pod," she yelled. "Starboard side." Then to me she added, "That's marine-speak for the right side of the vessel. The left side is called port."

I nodded as if I knew that because I didn't like the way she said it to me, as if I didn't.

The boat slowed down and it seemed as if all the people who had been inside were running out of the cabin and up the stairs to the viewing platform.

Black fins that looked like sharks' sliced

through the water directly toward us. They were all clumped together. "What did you call them?"

"They're orcas, also called killer whales. They live here in the Salish Sea. All the whales in a family that swim together are called a pod. This pod has Granny, the oldest killer whale. She's over a hundred years old!"

"But how can you tell which pod this is?"

"They all have a unique saddle patch on their dorsal fin."

I couldn't see the difference at all, except that some of the fins were longer than others. One of the orcas lifted its head out of the water and I glimpsed the white markings for a moment before it disappeared.

A gust of wind pushed me forward. The boat rocked harder with the waves and I gripped the railing to steady myself.

Almost everyone was up top taking pictures. I peered over to the other side of the boat, to the port side. The biggest whale I'd ever seen in

my life leaped out of the water, its body arched. Long fins on its side stuck out like airplane wings. It splashed back down with a loud slap.

"Humpbacks!" Marina squealed. "That was a juvenile breaching. A young one."

A line of mist suddenly shot out of the water, and I heard a sound like Grandpa blowing his nose real loud.

"The mom whale is coming beside it!" Marina hopped. "They're going to pass right in front of us!"

I caught a whiff of something like bad breath. Fishy. "That was a young one?"

"Yeah, adults are almost fifty feet. That's longer than a school bus!"

I couldn't believe our luck. I searched the cabin to see if Mom and Dad were watching, but I couldn't see them.

"I should go get my parents," I said.

"Where—?" But before she could finish, she gaped at something behind me, her eyes growing wide.

"DAD!" she screamed.

I didn't have time to look. The boat rocked violently out from under my feet, and then hurtled me into the air.

CHAPTER THREE

Darkness. Black and cold. I didn't know which way was up. How deep did I plunge? Weird hollow noises. Must get air!

Up, up, my suit pushed me up like a beach ball.

I broke the surface and gasped a loud sucking noise. Freezing water filled my lungs. I coughed and coughed.

Chaos.

Waves slammed my face. Wind screamed. The ocean spun around me. Cold water everywhere. Something shrieking. What was that noise?

"Mom!" I tried to yell, but my mouth filled with salty water. I gagged and wiped my eyes. Turning my head from the waves, I tried to look around. My breathing was fast and choppy. Something was in the water off to my right. What was that? A whale?

"The whale attacked the boat," someone behind me sobbed.

Waves crashed against the thing in the water. People screamed all around me.

"Help! I can't swim!"

"Hailey! Where's Hailey?"

"Dad!" I yelled, just as a wave broke over my head. I tried again, pushing myself higher in the water. "DAD!"

Where were they? Where was my sister?

Someone was climbing the thing in the water. I realized it was the bottom of the boat. It looked so wrong upside down. I flailed my arms, trying to swim closer.

"Get away from the boat," I heard someone yell. "It's going down."

"Help!" Someone close by yelled.

I turned and saw Marina barely bobbing on the surface. She was thrashing weakly with one arm, trying to twist her face away from going underwater. She moaned, holding her arm close to her body.

I spun back toward the boat, but heard Marina moan again. A wave broke over her face.

The panic cleared from my mind. I had to get her! I swam toward her and grabbed the back of her jacket.

She clung to me, screeching, "I can't move my arm."

The wind was blowing us farther away. There was something red in the water next to the boat. It grew on the surface like a balloon. People were helping each other climb in. A life raft.

"Come on," I said, trying to kick toward it. Cold waves washed over my face. The salt stung my eyes. I couldn't see. Suddenly, it seemed impossibly far to swim.

"Mom! Dad!" I yelled. "Stacey!"

"Hu-huddle with me," Marina said. "Get into the HELP position."

"What?" I yelled at her.

"Tuck your arms to your sides. Hug yourself. Bring your knees toward . . ." She coughed as a wave filled her mouth. ". . . chest. Keeps your heat in. Heat. Escape. Lessening. Position."

It was getting harder to hold her up. I kept kicking toward the life raft, but it was so far now. How did it get so far away?

"We have to kick toward the island," Marina said, nodding her head toward a small island behind us.

The wind and waves were pushing us in that direction, so it was easier to turn away from the waves that were breaking over my face. Something bumped me in the back. I screamed, thinking it was a whale.

Marina yelled, "Grab it!"

It was a long piece of plywood, just barely on the surface of the water. When we both grabbed it, it didn't sink far. It was such a relief to have something to hold on to.

Marina stretched across it as if it were a surfboard and started kicking toward the island. "Come on! Kick!"

I draped my body next to hers on the board, and we both kicked like motorboats. But it was tough to make the board go where we wanted. It was square and didn't move through the water well.

Waves crashed along the shoreline. Big splashes of water shot up from the rocks straight into the air. I kicked as hard as I've ever kicked in my life, but we were still too far away to swim to shore. The waves were going to sweep us past the tip of the island.

"Should we try to swim?" I yelled.

Marina shook her head. "Too much energy. And I think my wrist is broken."

My heart pounded in my head. I panted big gulps of air as we surfed on top of the waves. We sailed past the island and watched it go by. I didn't think I'd make the swim anyway.

"We lost too much body heat with all that kicking," Marina said. "Get as much of your skin out of the water as you can. The water sucks out your heat faster than the air."

We crawled farther up on the board, but it

started to sink with my weight. I slipped off a bit.

"Here, I'm wearing the suit, you stay on the board," I said. I craned my head as high as I could to look behind us. But I couldn't see over the waves. I'd lost sight of the boat and the life raft. I looked around at where we had drifted.

There was nothing but endless water. We were all alone out here.

CHAPTER FOUR

We weren't entirely alone. Long ships passed in the distance, too far away to see us.

"We have about an hour," Marina said. "Then we'll probably lose consciousness."

"What?" I didn't want to die. I started breathing faster again, searching around for my parents. For anyone.

"After you fall into cold water, a bunch of things happen. The big thing is, it makes you gasp. You can't help it. And if you're underwater, that's bad. The first minute is where you panic and hyperventilate. You breathe too fast and suck in water and drown."

We tucked in our chins as a wave pushed us from behind. I remembered panicking. But I saw Marina and it made me think about something else.

"But if you don't panic," she continued, "then you have about ten minutes to set up your life raft before you start to lose feeling in your fingers. Our arms are going to stop working properly."

Marina sounded like a robot. Wasn't she as scared as I was? I watched her face as she talked, and slid even closer to her on the board. Her calmness made me feel better.

She looked around. "Maybe we have more than an hour since we're out of the water, and wearing lots of layers." She glanced back at me. "And you'll last longer than me with that suit. Also, body fat insulates."

"I used to be good at gymnastics." I wanted

to explain I wasn't always like this. When I was on the team, I didn't have time to play Minecraft. But that was over a year ago. Now that's all I do.

"Dad must've released the life raft," Marina said, as if she didn't hear me. "Someone will spot that. He wouldn't have had time to radio a distress call, it happened so fast."

"What happened? What did you see?" I asked her. "Did the mom whale get angry and attack?"

I couldn't imagine a whale larger than the one that had jumped out of the water, but it would have to have been big to sink our big boat.

Marina looked at me then. "What? No, that's ridiculous. It was a rogue wave. The biggest monster I've ever seen. A wall of water hit us. And everyone was on the starboard side looking at the orcas. All the weight on the top deck and on one side . . ." She trailed off, looked like she was about to cry, then shook her head. "He's okay. He must have gotten in the life raft."

"My family too. They're all in the raft too, right?"

"I don't know. Probably." Marina looked above us. "Any minute we'll see the helicopter searching for us."

Every fourth or fifth wave was bigger than the others and broke behind our backs, then crashed on top of us. The board shot forward, then drifted, then shot forward again. We wobbled and splashed, trying to stay on top out of the water. Neither of us spoke, but I thought I could hear Marina sniffling.

My legs draped into the water and I kicked to keep us straight. I was glad now of the suit Mom had made me wear, though I could feel the cold water around my ankles. I rubbed my hand over my eyes. The salt water stung and caked my skin. It was all I could taste.

Marina held her right hand to her chest and clutched the board with her left.

"Does it hurt?" I asked.

Her expression slipped for a moment and she bit her lip. But she tossed her hair from her eyes and stared ahead. "When we make it to shore, we're going to need to build a fire right away. And a shelter."

She described how we were definitely going to make it to shore. And then how we'd make a shelter. How we would use it to get warm and how we'd need to build a signal fire for the rescuers to find us.

I nodded, but my thoughts raced along with my heart. Where were Mom and Dad? Did Stacey find them? Did they get in the raft? Were they looking for me right now? How would they find us out here? There was so much water. Nothing to see but curling, frothing waves in every direction. Splashing, crashing, endless.

The waves were like hills taller than me now. I threw my arm over Marina so she wouldn't be washed over. My fingers were cold and stiff. How long could we last out here?

"Twenty-five-knot wind," Marina mumbled. "Drifting about five knots with the current. Ebb tide." She was starting to sound weaker.

Was she going unconscious? I nudged her with my shoulder. "Keep talking to me. How come you know all this stuff?"

"Just Dad and me. Mom left when I was six. Dad was a commercial fisherman, but we could make a better living in the tourist industry. I take care of him. I learn about the whales. Going to be interpreter onboard tour boat. Teach people about marine life."

As I listened to her, my problems at home didn't seem so bad. At least my mom was around.

I lifted my head, got a hard wave in the face, wiped my eyes. I couldn't see the ships anymore. It looked like a cloud was tumbling over the mountains.

The wind howled behind us, screaming like a wild animal. It tried to tear us from the board. Waves smacked my back. But I started to become aware of another noise. It sounded like wet breathing.

It was right behind us.

I twisted but didn't see anything. What was that? I kicked to get away. The breathing returned, closer. I turned to look over one shoulder and then the other. And that's when I saw it.

A dark head with big eyes staring right at me.

CHAPTER FIVE

"Achh!" I splashed water at the thing. The head dove under.

"What?" Marina asked.

"There's something following us!" I yelled.

The head popped up again on my side of the board. It was so close I could see long nose slits. They opened wide, then closed. Its wet breathing sounded like a big, hissing snake.

"Harbor seal," Marina said. She smiled weakly and adjusted her grip so she could turn over and look at it.

"It's coming to watch over us. That makes

sense," she said. "Our boat's called the *Selkie*. That's a half seal, half person. It's a myth, like a unicorn. People in Scotland used to call them selkies."

The seal dove under.

Marina rolled back to her stomach. "Now we have our own protective selkie."

It didn't seem like it was protecting us.

It popped up again in front of us. The head was a sleek black with light gray specks and white whiskers. They were long and coarse, sticking straight out like the whiskers of a cat. Some poked up like eyebrows too.

I followed the whiskers down to meet the seal's gaze. Her big dark eyes were soft and sort of sad-looking. I felt like the seal was sorry this had happened to us. She was looking right into my eyes.

"She's not so bad." I hoped she would stay with us now. She made me feel better somehow. Like we weren't alone out here. I wished she could tow us to shore.

I looked around for the line of cliffs that marked the shore, but couldn't see it anymore. I couldn't see much of anything except a cloud. It had crept along the water and wrapped us up. It seemed like we were in our own world, and it had gotten a lot smaller.

"Fog. That's bad," Marina said. "Hard for Coast Guard to find us." Her lips had a blue tinge to them.

I flexed my fingers. They felt fat and awkward with cold. How long had we been out here bobbing on the waves? It felt like days.

"Got to get warm," Marina was saying.

She only had on the life vest over her coat, but I was wearing a thick, insulated suit with wide cuffs and a zipper up to the chin. "Do you want to wear this?" I said.

She shook her head. "Both of us drown. Keep it. Too hard to take off in water."

Her face was pale and she shivered violently. She wasn't looking good.

My heart started to pound again. How could I help her out here? When were the rescuers going to get here? Could they come in the fog? What was I supposed to do? Why was this happening to me?

The seal popped up next to me. She spun like a top and peeked at me, as if to check whether I was watching.

"Hi, seal. I'm watching. Stay with me."

She swam a little ahead, then came back to stare, then swam again out in front of me.

"You want me to chase you?" I kicked. My feet were so numb I could hardly feel them. "Wait up! I'm not as fast as you."

The seal swam ahead and I kicked to follow. She twisted, spun, and dove. She popped up next to me as if this were all a giant game. She made me smile. Gave me something to look at besides the dense fog and the endless waves. Made me forget to be scared.

The fog made the waves seem bigger. They

pounded me into the board, shoved us violently. Then I heard something ahead of us. Crashing like waves on a shore.

I kicked harder. Suddenly, tall trees appeared out of the fog like King Kong looming over us.

"Marina! There's the shore!"

"Rip current," she said quietly.

I kicked desperately toward it, but a strong current pushed us back. I used the last of my energy, pulling with one arm while gripping the board with the other. It looked like a river of foam between us and the shore. My arms and legs flailed madly. Still we were no closer. The current was too strong.

"Marina, help me kick!" My voice sounded faint behind the pounding in my ears.

There was no way I could get us in. My whole body vibrated with exhaustion. I gripped the board and leaned against Marina, taking in big gulps of air. We were going to drown twenty feet from shore.

Suddenly, Selkie popped up next to us again. I stopped fighting the current and drifted toward her. Her gaze drilled into me. She seemed to be telling me to find the strength to follow her again.

I let the current push me out, and then along the shoreline, following Selkie. I managed to kick a little as the waves battered us from the side. We crept farther along the shore, past the thick foam into a floating patch of kelp. Finally, the current stopped pushing us out. Selkie barked at me and then disappeared.

I struggled toward shore. We were going to make it!

Powerful waves picked us up and sucked us backward. I clutched the board and yelled. Then we were shoved forward, hurtling down the face of a wave. As we approached the shore, I stretched my feet toward bottom, but they didn't quite touch. Another wave sucked us back, then spit us closer. My feet dragged on gravel but I couldn't hold. We shot backward again and then forward, slamming hard onto the rocks. Marina cried out.

I clutched, scraped, clawed to get out of the water. It pulled, tried to yank us, but I fought it.

Marina struggled to get up. I grabbed her and pulled her with me. She still held the board as if she was frozen to it, or didn't want to give it up.

My legs shook so bad, I could hardly stand. In my desperation to get out of the water, I stumbled and fell. Waves and kelp pulled at my legs, my arms. The air felt warmer but the wind chilled my icy skin.

Had to stay onshore! No more cold ocean!

I dragged Marina and the board, tripping and flopping until we collapsed in a heap on top of a bunch of slimy, thick seaweed.

"We made it, Marina! We're saved."

I lifted my head and looked around for houses or cars or people. There were no houses or roads or docks. All I could see were rocks and trees.

"Help!" I screamed.

The only sound back was the roar of the surf.

CHAPTER SIX

"What should we do now? Where are we?" I asked.

No response. I turned. "Marina?"

She was curled in a ball where I'd left her. "Need warm" is all she said.

I helped her lean against a clump of bushes so she looked more comfortable. What had she said out on the water? We needed to start a fire and make a shelter. But how? "Marina, tell me again what to do."

She looked at me and shivered.

I scanned up and down the shoreline. Rock

walls on either side. We were lucky to have drifted to this spot; otherwise, we'd have been smashed against the cliff face. Waves crashed brutally onto the beach, flinging water high into the air. The rest of the water went on beyond the fog. How was there fog *and* wind?

There was a narrow strip of dirt and seaweed in a line about midway between the waves and a flat section of tall, swaying grasses. The forest loomed behind the grass.

I thought of all the times I wished my mom would leave me alone, stop babying me. All the times I wished my older sister hadn't been around. Now I wished so badly there were a grownup here. Anyone who would know what to do.

I looked at Marina again. I *did* know what to do. She had to get warm.

I yanked open the snaps on the front pockets of my suit. Nothing but an empty candy bar wrapper and a Ziploc bag with crumbs in it.

"Marina, do you have a lighter?"

"No." She trembled.

"Do you have anything we can use besides your knife?"

She gazed ahead, eyes unfocused. She had something in her pocket, but I couldn't clamp my thumb and fingers together hard enough to pull the zipper open. I realized I was shivering. My feet felt like blocks of ice. Both of us needed to get warm.

Coach used to make us do burpees to warm up. I dropped to the ground, my hands in the wet gravel as I did a pushup, then leaped up with my hands in the air. Again, down to the ground, push up, jump.

My heart started to pump; my breathing came faster. I hadn't done burpees since I quit the team. They were harder than I remembered. But it worked. I could feel and move my fingers. I yanked my zipper down and peeled off my suit. Kneeling next to Marina again, I pulled off the little vest she was wearing and helped her into my suit. It was wet, but still warm from my body heat.

She yelled when I tried to stuff her right arm into the sleeve. "M-my wrist!"

It looked swollen and sort of purple under the skin as she cradled it to her chest. When my friend Chad sprained his wrist breaking a fall on the mats, Coach wrapped it so it wouldn't move during the trip to the hospital.

Searching the ground next to us, I found two straight sticks and held them up next to her arm.

"Hold these," I said. "You don't have any tape, do you?"

Then I got an idea. I ripped the lace out of my right shoe and tied the sticks with that. Marina still had her bandanna around her neck. I reached under her hair. The knot was wet and hard to undo, but I got the bandanna free and laid it out in a triangle like Coach had done with a piece of cloth from the first-aid kit. I cradled Marina's arm in that and tied the bandanna around her neck so that her fingers pointed up next to her collarbone. "Does that feel better?"

"Fire," she mumbled.

I searched through the pocket of her vest. My hand pulled out a plastic bag with a lighter and a small box of matches in it.

"Yes!" I cheered, until I took a closer look at what I had thought was a lighter. It was just a black rectangular block the size and weight of a lighter.

What was this thing? Why couldn't this be a lighter? I hated matches. I could never work them.

The little box of matches was dry from being in the bag, but it stuck when I tried to slide it open. The box slipped from my fingers and most of the matches fell into the mud.

"No!" I lunged for the box and collected the few matches that weren't wet. More carefully, I pulled out one of the matches that were still in the box. "The box says they're waterproof, so it should work, right?"

I tried to rub the match head along the side of the box. The thin matchstick broke in my fingers. I threw it to the ground and tried another one. Again.

There weren't that many dry matches left. I crouched on the ground and carefully laid the match along my finger so it wouldn't break, but when I dragged it along the strike strip nothing happened. I had never understood the coordination it takes to make matches work.

"Argh!" I yelled in frustration.

I looked up in surprise when I felt a splash. I'd been so focused on the matches, I hadn't noticed what was going on around me. My attention now traveled along the line of seaweed and sticks. The ground above that line was a lighter color than the side closer to the ocean. Now I understood that this was how high the tide came up. And we weren't on the right side of the line.

Calm down. I had to concentrate. And I had to get ready to light the fire. I didn't have anything prepared to burn. I needed to stop panicking and think. What had Marina said about how much time we had before we'd get hypothermia? If I didn't get this fire started, we were both going to die.

I helped her crawl above the seaweed line to an area that was level with some boulders. Then I crouched behind the biggest boulder and scraped a bare patch in the dirt. I piled some twigs and driftwood that I found lying between the rocks and then I crouched over the pile and pulled out another match. I flicked it quick across the box and it made a snapping sound like when Dad lit matches. It worked!

The wind blew behind me and puffed it out.

I could feel myself starting to panic again. We needed to get warm right now. I tried again and again until I had one match left.

I focused on the match. Pressed my lips together, lined up the matchstick against my finger.

This was it.

This one would work. I had the hang of it now.

I flicked it across the matchbox. The match head flared up bright. And then died. I was left with nothing but a smoking match and darkness falling fast.

CHAPTER SEVEN

Marina pointed at the bag on the ground with shaking hands. "Mag. Magnes. Inside."

I pulled out the block I had thought was a lighter.

Marina made sawing motions. "S-shave. On tinder." She gestured weakly.

I peered closer and saw there were little cotton balls inside the baggie. What was she talking about? "This black stuff will light the balls on fire?"

Marina closed her eyes and sank into the coat.

"Marina. Don't leave me here alone. I need help!"

No response.

"Marina!" I leaned toward her. My heart pounded as I tried to hear hers. *Please let her stay alive.* I pressed my ear to her nose. I sighed when I felt and heard her breath.

Then I studied the block, turning it over in my hands. It looked like one side had been gouged away by a knife or something, and the other side had a black stripe down it like the matchbox. The cotton balls dropped onto my small pile of sticks when I shook out the bag. They were coated in some kind of goo.

I pulled Marina's knife from its sheath. When I saw it on the boat, I never would have guessed I'd be using it.

I scraped the knife down the side of the block and little pieces came off that looked like metal shavings. I pushed harder on the knife with the blade facing up, and dragged it along the block toward my foot. More pieces came off. Then I

flipped over the block and studied the stripe
again.

How did this light a fire? I tapped it with
the knife and was surprised when a little spark
flared off it.

"Whoa!" I looked at the knife in my hand,
then back at the block.

Holding the block up, I struck it with the
knife again, harder. This time a shower of bright
sparks came off. This was easier than thin, small

matches; the knife wasn't going to snap in my fingers.

After a few tries, I figured out how to aim the sparks onto the shavings. They burst into flames, and then the cotton balls ignited.

I sat back, stunned. "I made a fire!"

I turned to Marina. "Hey, look! I made this!"

I dropped the block and put my hand in front of her nose again. Still breathing.

The flames were starting to die. I put more sticks on top and the flames caught. Pretty soon, the fire was crackling and popping and the heat bounced off the boulder toward us. I held my palms toward it and smiled. But my smile faded as I looked up. Darkness was falling fast.

"Are they going to find us at night, Marina?"

Relief crashed through me when she opened her eyes, but she said nothing. We looked at each other over the smoke of the fire. She looked scared. I remembered how scared I was in the ocean and how her calmness had helped me feel better.

"Don't worry," I said, forcing my voice to sound relaxed. "I'm going to make us a shelter. We're going to survive the night. And then the rescuers will come." I wasn't sure about any of it, but it looked like Marina needed to hear it.

I tried to picture what our tent looked like when we set it up in the yard. Back when Stacey used to do cool things like that with me.

"I need a long branch to use as a ridgepole," I told Marina. "I'll be right back."

Racing toward the forest, I searched the ground as I went. I brought all the things I gathered back to the fire and piled them next to Marina. As I worked, I kept talking.

"We have to make sure we don't set up next to an ant nest. I made that mistake before. Stacey had ants crawling up her legs and biting her inside her pajamas! You should have heard her screaming! It was hilarious. But let's not do that tonight."

There was another boulder near the fire that was as high as my chest. We were above the tide line here, and the ground was dry. I propped one end of the long bare branch I'd found against the top of the boulder with the other end on the ground. Then I leaned the board we had brought to shore with us against the branch so it looked like one side of a tent.

I had to stop to add more wood to the fire. "I don't like the dark," I told Marina. "Not since I had to sit in a dark room for two whole days. No TV, no computer, no games. It sucked."

I didn't tell her the other thing I was even more afraid of than the dark.

For the other side of the shelter, I used pieces of driftwood, and then filled in the spaces between the driftwood with dried seaweed and smaller branches. Once it was done, it looked like a lumpy lean-to, with the opening facing the fire and the ocean. I bent and crawled in. There was enough room to turn and lie down with my feet at the narrow end and my head just inside. Though it looked dry, the ground was uneven and damp.

It was almost too dark to see. Mosquitoes whined in my ears. I brushed them away and raced back to the forest to collect armfuls of leaves. I brought them to the shelter and threw them inside. Then I pulled branches off trees, the kinds with lots of needles on them. Needles and cobwebs and mosquitoes stuck to my neck and face. I swatted at the bugs and ran back toward the light of the campfire.

"This is our mattress," I told Marina as I arranged the branches on top of the leaves. I could see with the light of the fire. The mosquitoes weren't as bad around the smoke.

"Come on." I pulled Marina up and helped her slide in feet first. With the fire in front of us and the walls up, the heat from the fire filled the little shelter. After collecting more firewood, I crawled in next to Marina.

Once I stopped moving, I heard the quiet the waves had left in their wake. Instead of crashing, now they barely made a noise like frying eggs as they hissed up and down the

gravel. An owl hooted somewhere behind us and I tensed.

"Marina, are you awake yet?"

She mumbled.

I needed someone to talk to so that bad thoughts wouldn't come. The noises were scary out here, not at all like our backyard with the porch light on and the sound of the neighbors' TV and of cars driving by.

Suddenly, I heard a loud spray burst out of the ocean.

"What?" I yelped.

Then I recognized the blowing noise I'd heard on the whale tour boat, and my racing heart calmed. I threw more wood on the fire, and watched the sparks rise into the black toward the stars.

I lay back down. "Tomorrow, rescuers are going to find us — right, Marina?"

No answer.

The sounds of the humpbacks breathing kept me company.

CHAPTER EIGHT

I woke to the sound of barking.

"What—?" Marina said. Her voice was hoarse. She'd been puking in the night, but I must've fallen back asleep.

I stumbled out of the shelter. It was still too dark to figure out what the weird shadows were on the beach. When my eyes adjusted I saw that the tide had slid up to the rocks.

Bark-bark-bark.

"Hello?" I yelled, hoping there were rescuers with dogs. I started toward the shore but stopped short when I saw what the noise was coming from.

"You found me," I said. "And you brought your friends."

"Huh?" Marina said from the shelter, louder.

Two dark, hulking outlines wriggled into the water with a splash. I gazed out at the sleek heads bobbing in the ocean. I was sure I recognized that mottled one with gray specks. She let out a loud bark when she saw me and dove under.

"Seals," I told her. "Selkie is checking up on us."

My tongue felt glued to the roof of my mouth. A throbbing pain pulsed at my temples and my throat ached.

Marina rolled over slowly to peer out of the shelter. "Where are the rescuers? They need to find us. I can't stay here."

My suit was draped over her like a blanket after she'd taken it off during the night. Her lips were cracked and peeling, and her hair was matted to one side of her head. She looked like she was about to cry.

We both desperately needed water. I looked at all the water in the ocean next to us. All the wet noises from the seals splashing around were making me crazy. But I knew from those salty waves crashing into my face that we couldn't drink any of it.

"We must be out of the search grid," Marina wailed. "Remember that island we missed? What if they don't find us? My arm hurts. I'm so thirsty. If we don't find water, we're going to die."

I stared at her. What had happened to the robot girl from yesterday? Her freak-out was making me freak out. I could feel my pulse speeding up. I needed breakfast. I needed to know where my parents were. I needed to go home.

I saw the blackened fire pit. It reminded me

of that feeling I had last night when I lit the fire. I had felt in control. We needed to get warm, and I had done it. If I figured out that problem, I could tackle this one, too.

"We need to stop and think," I said. "Where would we find water?"

Marina was too busy peeking under the bandanna at her wrist. It was as if I were the older one now. "I'll go find a stream," I said.

But after searching the thick forest behind the shelter, all I found were spider webs, an old tire, and a long white balloon, the kind they use to drape over the sides of boats to keep them from banging into things.

I also found a plastic water bottle, but it was empty. I licked my dry lips. The pounding in my head got worse.

When I stepped out of the forest, I noticed that all the grasses were bent over and wet with dew. I licked one, and the moisture felt so good in my mouth. I looked at the empty bottle in my hand and then at the grasses covered in water. If only there was a way to get the dew into the bottle.

I shrugged out of my sweater and tore off my shirtsleeve. Then I used the sleeve as a rag to mop up the dew. I squeezed the rag over the bottle and it began to fill. It took a while, but I managed to collect almost a quarter of a bottle. I brought it carefully back to the shelter. Marina was still huddled under my suit. When she turned and saw me, her eyes went big. "Oh!"

I was proud of the way she looked at me then. Not like I was someone who didn't know port from starboard.

"How's your arm?" I asked, handing her the open bottle.

She took a drink, measured how much was left, then took another small sip. "I'm really sick. It's making me scared." She wiped her mouth and ducked her head.

"I get scared too," I said. "I'm the most scared person of anyone I know."

"About what?" She handed me the rest of the water.

I thought of my parents and sister, of my gut worry over whether they got into the life raft, but couldn't talk about any of that.

"I was on the gymnastics team." I started gathering more sticks for a fire. "My friend Chad and I dared each other to do a giant swing on the high bar. You're not supposed to go on the bar without Coach to spot you, but we snuck in. I landed on my head and got a concussion. For two days I had to sit in a dark room to heal my brain. Since then, my mom treats me like I'm about to fall on my head again any minute."

"So you're afraid of gymnastics? Is that why you're not on the team anymore?"

I stopped scraping the black block with the knife. I'd never told anyone why. "What is this?" I held the block out to her.

"This is magnesium. The scrapings burn quick and hot. You can light fires if you don't have matches."

"Yeah," I said, striking the knife against the block.

I sighed. "I guess I didn't realize how high the horizontal bar was. I couldn't do any of it after the accident. Not the rings, not the vault, not even the horse. Floor wasn't my best event, so I quit. I can hardly climb stairs now. If I go too high, I start to shake and feel all fluttery."

Marina paused, eyeballing me. Finally she gestured at the fire. "We need green branches." She looked calmer now, not so freaked. I was relieved to see her eyes focus. It must've helped her to hear about other people being scared.

"Green?" I asked.

"Live branches to put on the fire. It makes smoke. We have to be ready to signal when the helicopters come." She licked her lips. "And we need more water."

My stomach growled so loud, we both looked around. Our eyes met and she gave me a shaky smile. "Food, too, I guess."

"My pocket." I pointed to the immersion suit on the ground next to her. "Animal crackers," I said as she pulled out the Ziploc bag.

"You thought of everything," she said.

We both dipped our fingers into the crumbs and licked them off. It didn't make me any less hungry. Then I looked at the bag I'd left on the ground yesterday. It had a few drops of condensation in it. It reminded me of something Stacey had done in eighth grade.

"Hey, we can use this to make a solar still."

"A what?"

"My sister had to do a school project for environmental science. Something to do with clean energy. I was surprised she was so smart, but then she told me she had read about it online."

I laid out the plastic bags we had. One large one from Marina's pocket and two small ones from mine. "If we fill these bags with plants, something green, and leave them in the sun,

they sweat inside. We can make our own water to drink!"

Marina grinned. "That *is* smart!"

I found clean stones and put one in a corner of each bag with the leaves and then carefully laid them out in the sun. The water would collect at the lowest point, where the stones were, and I could add water to the bottle again.

During the day we waited, ready with the fire. But there were no rescue helicopters overhead. No boats coming to get us. We saw big ships passing through the mouth of the strait, but they were far away.

"How are they going to find us if they don't come close enough to see our smoke?" I asked.

Marina craned her head to look up. She'd been drinking most of the water we got out of the solar stills, but she was still sick. She needed to go to a hospital.

"I don't know," she replied. "In the course I took, they just told us how not to drown. In all the stories, people who didn't drown got rescued. But they'd better hurry; we can't live much longer on dew. We can die from dehydration easier than drowning."

I wished she'd stop talking about dying every two minutes.

An eagle flew over us.

"There's another one," Marina said, scanning the tops of the trees. The eagle landed on a branch, the white of its head stark against the backdrop of the forest. It stared down at us. "I wonder if . . ." She perked up. "There! I knew it! We're saved!"

"What? Is it the helicopter? Where?" I stood up so fast I got dizzy.

"An eagle nest. This is where they set up the new cam. Now I know where we are! Wow, we're farther up the Cape than I thought. We'll never be able to walk to town. It's too far."

"What are you talking about? What's a cam?"

"There's a camera in that tree. The DNR just put it up so people could watch the eagles being born. All you have to do is go up there and signal."

She looked at me then with dismay because she had just remembered my confession.

My gaze ran up the height of the tree. At the same time, my stomach sank. It was so high.

"I can't," I whispered.

CHAPTER NINE

"Well, I can't do it." Marina pointed to her arm.

I thought of all I had done since the boat had gone over. About being in the water, and pulling Marina onto the board, and then getting to the shore. I had made a fire on my own. I never thought I could do that. I did it when I wasn't busy thinking I couldn't. I just did it. Seemed to me, the thing about surviving something is believing you can.

I looked way up the tree. All the way to the big ball of branches that Marina said was a nest.

"What about the eagles? Aren't they going to attack me?"

Marina shrugged. "I don't know. I've never climbed into an eagle's nest before."

"Well, that doesn't help."

"Maybe you should wear this. For protection?" She pointed to my immersion suit.

Slowly I pulled the suit on. My legs already felt wobbly and I hadn't even started climbing yet.

"There's no sound, just a camera, so don't bother talking," she called after me. "I'm also not sure if it's on all the time. I know they had to shut it down because of damage to the cables. Just jiggle it to make sure it's working. And hurry, it's going to get dark soon."

"Great," I muttered.

I stood beneath the lowest branch of the tree. It was like the highest parallel bars I'd ever seen. The lowest branch was way too far up to make it in a simple leap. I needed a springboard to mount.

I searched around and found a log with a broken end. I rolled it toward the tree and then propped it up on the trunk under the first branch. It wedged itself in as I shook it. Now all I had to do was run up the log and leap to that branch. The thought made me feel sick.

I stared up again, trying to judge the distance. Trying to ignore the pounding in my chest.

I rubbed my shaking hands on my suit, then clapped them together as if I were pounding off the chalk. I slowly backed up, moving branches out of the way. A simple move I'd done a million times. Except not nearly so high. Could I even reach that branch? What if I missed?

Don't think. Just do.

I took off at a sprint, ran straight up the log, and used my speed to leap into the air, swinging my arms over my head to give my jump more momentum. I stretched out my fingers as far as they would go, reaching, reaching.

I caught the branch with the tips of my fingers and somehow clung on. It was rough under my hands, and my skin scraped as I hung. I swung my legs upward and aimed for the next branch. Don't look down. That's all. Just keep climbing.

Of course, as soon as I thought about not looking down, I looked. The ground swayed beneath me. So far below already. I imagined it rushing up toward me, remembered the hollow sound, the last thing I heard before everything went black.

Stop thinking! Focus on the task. If I could keep my thoughts on just the climb, there would be no room for panic.

I pulled myself higher. Reached, stretched to the next branch, and the next one. My muscles trembled but they knew the motions. It was as if my arms and legs had their own mind and just did it. Stretch, reach, lunge, grasp, pull.

The bark left the skin on my palms raw, but I ignored it. Must keep going up. Branches started getting thinner closer to the top. But the worst part was the swaying. The tree swayed with the breeze up here, and with my weight. Every time I moved, the tree swayed more. My heart hammered in my chest.

Thump thump thump.

I could feel my pulse in the scratches on my face and hands. Finally, I was underneath the mass of sticks that was the nest. But that's when I realized what the hard part was going to be.

The nest was like a shallow bowl sitting in the center of a cluster of branches. It was as wide across as I was tall. I was going to have to reach far out to get around and over it.

Carefully, I pulled myself along the underside of the nest, grabbing the sticks and branches that stuck out. The muscles in my arms screamed as I hung sideways; my whole body shook. Slowly, I raised my head and peered inside. *Please let the camera be working.*

When my eyes came level with the nest, I was met by three angry heads. They shrieked and glared at me as I crawled onto the nest.

Blink. Blink.

"I'm just borrowing your camera," I whispered to them. "Don't call your mom and dad!"

I was expecting fuzzy chicks—*small* chicks. They were almost the same size as an adult eagle, but they didn't have the white heads. And they acted like babies. They huddled together, taking up most of the space.

The nest was big enough to sleep on. In fact, it looked more comfortable than the shelter I had made. Except for the dried-up carcass of something long dead. That explained the smell.

The camera was there on a branch, but I had no idea if it was working. I wasn't sure what I was expecting. Maybe for the screen to be like Stacey's camera phone, where you could see yourself. This camera was just a green, square box with a hood over the lens. I waved my arms in front of it while balancing on the branch.

"Help!" I yelled at it, before I remembered there was no sound. I swung my arms around and tried to show how we swam from the boat,

hugged a board, rode the waves onto this shore, and then how I made fire to dry us off and warm us.

All the while the chicks blinked at me, staring. I kept looking over my shoulder, terrorized by the thought of an adult eagle swooping down on me. Any second I expected to see the large wingspan.

Could they peck out my eyes? Most definitely they'd claw at me. Push me out of the nest. I'd fall down, down, down from the bar.

No. I wasn't on the bar. I was in a tree. And darkness was coming. I had to get down while it was still light enough to see.

I moved and a twig snapped. All three eaglets startled and started to screech. I heard loud wind sounds like flapping, and looked up to see two huge eagles circling over me. They both screamed back.

I craned my head looking up, but leaned out too far. My arms windmilled, and then I toppled off the nest.

CHAPTER TEN

I fell with a sickening feeling. My arms flailed wildly. Hands clutched, trying to grab something.

I caught a branch under my knee, missed the grip, and fell to the next one. I slammed into the branch but grabbed hold and stuck.

I hung from the branch, my body dangling. Then I pulled myself up and hugged the tree trunk. Pulse pounding.

Opening my eyes, I saw I had only dropped a short distance. I was still high in the tree. I was still alive! But I needed to get down.

I dropped from branch to branch, first carefully placing each hand, and then letting myself swing and hang. I had to trust my body. I was a gymnast and I could do this.

An eagle screamed above me. I glanced up and missed my next hold. I slipped. A branch caught me under the left arm and stopped me short. I clung tightly, breathing hard. Rough bark digging in. Focus!

Branch by branch, I made my way toward the ground. When I got to the lowest branch, I peered down at the log I had braced against the tree. How had I jumped that high? I couldn't let myself drop that far.

I sat on the branch, both legs dangling over the side. What was I going to do? I was stuck in the tree.

If I slid down the trunk with bare hands, I'd be flayed alive by the rough bark.

I patted my pockets and took a closer look at the belt on the suit. It was made with a wide band that looked like seat belt material. I pulled it out of the loops until I was holding just the belt, and then expanded it so it was as long as possible. Now I needed to get it around the tree trunk. I tried whipping it so the end would come around the trunk, but it didn't reach all the way. I kept trying to whip the buckle around the tree until, finally, I was able to grab it with my other hand.

I had both ends in my hands now. I just needed to jump. When I peered down at the ground, it swayed. I shut my eyes tight.

"Be brave. Let yourself go. You used to do this. You can do it again."

I eased my butt off the branch. Bracing my feet against the trunk, I leaned out, clinging to the belt. My stomach leaped up into my throat with the feeling of falling. I slid down the trunk, bark flying from my shoes. Before I'd even shut my eyes, the belt stopped short on the propped log and I let go. I dropped the rest of the way and landed.

Not on my head. On my feet.

I raised my arms and posed like I had just struck a perfect landing. My knees trembled; my legs hardly held me. I craned my head to look up into the branches.

"Yeah, I can!" I yelled.

"Did it work?" Marina shouted back. "Are they coming?"

"They're coming!" I yelled as I raced back to our camp. I could see the fire burning bright against the dimming light.

But no one came.

As darkness settled, we had to face another night in the shelter. Mosquitoes and black flies crawled in my hair, buzzed in my ears. Marina's wrist was now twice as swollen as it had been, and a really ugly color. And we were thirsty. I was feeling even worse after all that climbing.

"You're going to have to walk out of here and let them know where I am," she said quietly. "I can't walk that far."

The night was long.

I added wood to the fire to keep the bugs away. We listened to the whales and the seals and the owls and things that scurried in the dark behind us. Each new noise made us freeze and stare, wide-eyed, into the night.

Soon, the forest around us appeared in the pre-dawn light. We were still planning how I was going to be able to find help. How to follow the shoreline so I wouldn't get lost. I didn't want to leave Marina.

Once again, we heard splashes coming from the ocean. "Selkie coming to check on us?" I said, as I rolled over.

"Not seals," Marina said.

I looked out and my whole body zinged with energy. We turned to each other and laughed. And then Marina started to cry. She held out her good arm and we hugged.

A boat was coming straight toward us.

CHAPTER ELEVEN

Back home four months later

"There were dozens of calls," the reporter said, as I finished my story. He chuckled. "Complaints to the Department of Natural Resources about 'the kid in the tree' disturbing the eagles." He sat back. "Did you know that?"

"I heard." I took a big drink of my lemonade. Telling the story—just remembering it all—made me thirsty.

"Thank goodness for those nature lovers." Dad grinned from the loveseat next to me. "I'd never even heard of eagle cams before this. Who knew?"

"Well, thank goodness for the eagles," Mom said, placing a plate of cookies on the coffee table. "And for DNR for putting it up."

Dad reached to take her hand. She still got upset when I talked about it.

"I'm actually glad the whale attack rumors weren't true," the reporter said, earning a glare from Mom.

"Getting attacked by a whale wasn't the story here," he continued. "The real story is how you managed to not panic, save yourself, and save Marina, too!"

"We saved each other." I grabbed a cookie, still warm from the oven, and bit into it. The peanut butter center was gooey, my favorite. "I wouldn't have made it without Marina."

The reporter scratched his head with a pencil. "One thing I don't understand," he said. "You kept referring to yourself as overweight. You're obviously not."

"That was sixth grade. I'm back on the gymnastics team now. Coach says I 'got back on the horse.' He means the pommel horse. He thinks he's funny."

"And what about Marina? How was her wrist?"

"Oh, yeah. Broken. But she's better now. We video chat once a week. She's going to come to Ohio with her dad for a visit. We're both going to be marine biologists."

The grownups exchanged glances as if I weren't in the room. I knew they thought I sounded like a kid. But how could they understand I was serious? Having a seal look you in the eyes changes you.

"Wow, sounds like you have everything figured out," said the reporter.

"Dude," Stacey said as she stuck her head

into the room. "Dishwasher needs to be unloaded and it's your turn. I am *not* doing it."

I turned back to the reporter. "I haven't got everything figured out. Who can understand big sisters?"

AUTHOR'S NOTE

There have been numerous tragedies in the ocean around Washington's Cape Flattery and Canada's Vancouver Island. The area has a list of hazards that make it complicated to forecast the weather accurately. Currents, undercurrents, near-shore currents, reverse currents, tides, prevailing winds, upwelling, and freshwater runoff are all factors that boat operators need to consider.

The area also has sizable waves coming from the Pacific Ocean at the mouth of the Strait of Juan de Fuca, and when they come against the direction of the current, it creates dangerous standing waves. Not only that, but something known as rogue waves—unpredictable walls of water that develop out at sea—can surprise boaters in calm waters.

The waters in this area are part of what is known as the California Current System, a current of cold water that reaches from Alaska down to California. Cold, deep, nutrient-rich water upwells in the summer months, attracting marine life—including whales—with an abundance of food. Commercial fishermen, sailors, and sightseeing tours all share the waters. But immersion in water colder than fifty degrees is dangerous for humans, and boaters must be cautious.

Even with all those odds, there are many stories of survival. I was amazed to read about a woman who fell off a boat in the Puget Sound area and swam for seven hours before she was found and plucked from the water by a passing boat. She credited her survival to the company of a seal who stayed with her for the whole ordeal. The one thing most survivors have in common is the will to keep going. That is what fascinated and inspired me to write this story.

While this story was inspired by true events, and every effort was made to keep to the facts, some details are fictional, including the names of the characters and some settings, as well as the presence of an eagle cam in the particular location of Cape Flattery. (There *are* eagle cams in the Puget Sound area.)

SO, WHAT CAN YOU DO TO SURVIVE IF YOU FIND YOURSELF IN A SIMILAR SITUATION?

U.S. COAST GUARD–APPROVED COLD-WATER SURVIVAL TIPS

Every minute counts in cold water.

1. MINIMIZE YOUR TIME IN THE WATER.

Act quickly. Your body loses heat twenty-five times faster in the water than on land, so get out of the water as fast as you can.

2. GET TO A SURVIVAL CRAFT.

Board a boat, raft, or anything floating. Turn a capsized boat over and climb in. Remember, most boats will support you even when they are full of water. If you can't get in the boat, climb on top of it and stay with it. That way, it will be easier for a rescue boat to spot you on the water.

3. STAY CALM.

Flailing around in the water causes the body to lose heat faster. If you don't have an exposure suit, hold your knees to your chest to protect your trunk from heat loss, and clasp your arms around your calves. This is called HELP (the Heat Escape Lessening Position).

4. SAVE YOUR ENERGY.

Wearing a life jacket will help you save energy and will keep your body temperature from dropping quickly. Minimize the motion needed to keep afloat by helping to insulate the body.

5. KEEP YOUR CLOTHES ON.

Button, buckle, and zip up, and tighten collars, cuffs, shoes, and hoods. Wear a warm hat, like a fleece-lined skullcap, that will stay on your head in the water. Dress in layers of synthetic fabrics such as polyester fleece to keep from getting overheated or chilled from perspiration.

6. STAY PUT. DON'T TRY TO SWIM.

Don't try to swim unless your destination is very close. Ignore the shoreline; it is usually farther away than people think. Swimming disrupts the layer of warm water between your clothing and your body and sends the "warm" blood to your extremities, which cuts your survival time by as much as half.

7. DO THE HYPOTHERMIA HUDDLE.

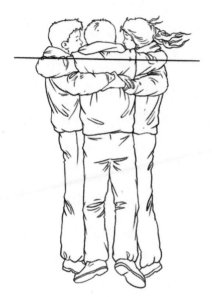

To preserve body heat, use the Heat Escape Lessening Position if you're alone, or if you're with a group, huddle with others. Rescuers are more likely to see you and rescue you faster if you're in a group.

Hypothermia

Though cold-water survival times vary from person to person, the colder the water is, the sooner hypothermia will set in. The likelihood of survivability is affected by the weather conditions and by a person's age, gender, weight, height, body fat percentage, fatigue level, immersion level, type of clothing worn, and survival gear available.

Recognizing Hypothermia

In the first stages of hypothermia, people can experience shivering, impaired judgment, clumsiness, and loss of dexterity.

In the later stages of hypothermia, body systems slow and eventually stop. Slurred speech, withdrawn behavior, muscle rigidity, and a cessation of shivering are signs of late hypothermia.

If left untreated, hypothermia will result in unconsciousness and death.

Treating Hypothermia

Rapid treatment of hypothermia is critical. If you identify someone as hypothermic, here's what you can do:

1. Call for help (call 911 or VHF-FM marine radio).

2. Restore warmth slowly.

3. Begin CPR (if necessary) while warming the person.

4. Give warm fluids.

5. Keep the person's temperature up by keeping him or her wrapped in a blanket.

Survival tips courtesy of the United States Coast Guard.

ACKNOWLEDGMENTS

In my research for writing this book, I collected information from many sources, including books, reports, and transcripts. I received helpful advice from a number of people, for which I am very grateful. Any errors in the story are my own.

I am grateful for the specialized advice I received from the following:

U.S. Coast Guard, Sector Puget Sound; Tammi Hinkle, Adventures Through Kayaking, Port Angeles, Washington; and Bruce Tomlinson, retired Ontario conservation officer of thirty years, Marine Enforcement Unit, Ministry of Natural Resources and Forestry.

Thank you to those who read the manuscript and provided excellent suggestions: Sylvia Musgrove, Jackie White, Marcia Wells, and Amy Fellner Dominy.

Thanks also go to Chris White and Steven White for reading the manuscript and giving me their expert opinions on where the illustrations should go.

ABOUT THE AUTHOR

Terry Lynn Johnson has lived in northern Ontario, Canada, for more than forty years. She grew up at the edge of a lake, where her parents owned a lodge. A nature enthusiast, she has explored Lake Huron with her family on their twenty-six-foot sailboat and has traveled more than two thousand kilometers on kayak expeditions in the Great Lakes, Alaska, and Nova Scotia.

She is a certified canoe instructor, and as the owner and operator of a dog-sledding business with eighteen huskies, she guided overnight trips and slept in quinzees.

She currently works as a conservation officer with the Ontario Ministry of Natural Resources and Forestry in the Northern Marine Enforcement Unit. She has seventeen years of hands-on experience and training working in cold-water marine environments and remote areas. She has trained with the Canadian Coast Guard and is qualified to operate vessels weighing up to sixty tons. Before becoming a conservation officer, she worked for twelve years as a canoe ranger warden in Quetico Wilderness Park.

In her free time, Terry enjoys snowshoeing, hiking, and dreaming up new ways to survive in the outdoors.

Here's a sneak peek at the next book in the
SURVIVOR DIARIES series: ***AVALANCHE!***

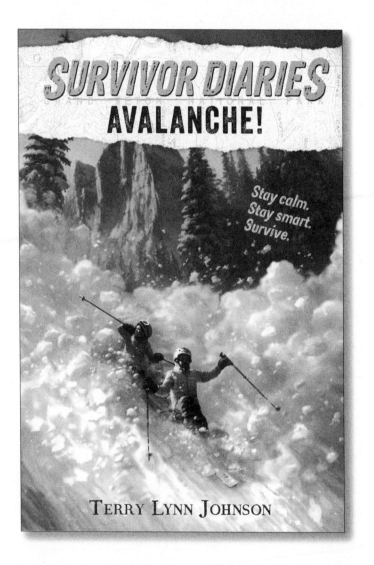

CHAPTER ONE

"Tell me how you survived the avalanche," the reporter said. He placed his phone on the kitchen table between us, then pressed Record. With his pen poised over his notepad, he looked at me expectantly. He smelled like grass and ink and summer tomatoes from the garden.

Without thinking, I glanced around for my brother, but he wasn't in sight.

"You sure you don't want to talk to Ryan, too?" Dad asked the reporter, filling his cup with coffee. "He's got a good eye for detail."

"Maybe later." The reporter smiled at me.

One tooth along the top was slightly crooked and stuck out. "I want to hear it from Ashley first."

"The avalanche wasn't even the worst part," I began. "But I'll never forget the roar. How fast it all happened. One minute we were skiing, the next we were being swept down the mountain at lightning speed. It just grabbed us and I couldn't stop myself from falling. I couldn't breathe. The snow was everywhere, a choking white blizzard in the air. Couldn't see—"

"Wait." The reporter stopped recording. "I explained to your parents, Ashley. I'm writing a series about brave kids like you who have survived in the wilderness. Readers will want to know everything you were thinking, everything you did, so they can learn what to do if it happens to them. Where were you? How did it happen? And why were you there? Try to tell me everything you remember."

He didn't look at Dad or anyone else. Only me.

I felt suddenly anxious about being part of a series about brave kids. I was used to just being Ashley Hilder, twelve years old, twin sister to the awesome Ryan Hilder. I had never been anything special before compared to him.

The reporter pressed the red Record button again. "Tell me your story."

I sat back in my chair, trying to conjure up the memory of that day. "It all started with the wolverines."

Stay calm. Stay smart. Survive.

Watch out for more books in the
SURVIVOR DIARIES series at survivordiaries.com!

SURVIVOR DIARIES

Do you have the smarts, the grit,
and the courage to survive?

—or—

Are you better off staying home?

YOU'VE READ THE BOOK, NOW PLAY THE GAME

WILL YOU SURVIVE?

www.survivordiaries.com